D1028993

# the Monsters
# Three

To Jimmy & Simon,
BOO!

2014

# the MONSTERS THREE

by Rosalind Bunn
& Kathleen Howard

illustrated by Lydia Rupinski

Kathleen Howard

Rosalind Bunn

Text © 2014 Rosalind Bunn & Kathleen Howard

Illustrations © 2014 Lydia Rupinski

ALL RIGHTS RESERVED - No part of this book may be reproduced in any form or by any electronic or mechanical means, including information storage and retrieval systems, without permission in writing from the authors, except by a reviewer who may quote brief passages in a review.

This is a work of fiction. Names, places, characters, and incidents are either products of the authors' imagination or are used fictitiously. Any resemblance to actual events, locales, persons, or characters, living or dead, is entirely coincidental.

Published by Deeds Publishing, Marietta, GA
www.deedspublishing.com

Printed in The United States of America
Library of Congress Cataloging-in-Publications Data is available upon request.

ISBN 978-1-941165-30-0

Typesetting and book design by Deeds Publishing

Books are available in quantity for promotional or premium use. For information, write Deeds Publishing, PO Box 682212, Marietta, GA 30068 or email info@deedspublishing.com.

First Edition, 2014


10 9 8 7 6 5 4 3 2 1

*To our own little monsters*
*who are all grown up*
*and to our Moms*
*who taught us*
*that manners matter*

We are the
MONSTERS THREE,
my two friends and me.
Halloween is our favorite time.
We go to get treats,
we say a rhyme.

We don't even care if we give a good scare.
The moon is full and the street is a sight.
We knock at the first door to begin our night.

We scream and we shout with all our might.
"WE WANT TO TRICK! WE NEED A TREAT!
WE WOULD EVEN LET YOU
SMELL OUR FEET!"

With treats in hand,
we turn and we run.
To the next house we go
to continue the fun.

We push and we shove
when we get to the door,
not saying excuse me
or pardon
our roar.

"WE WANT TO TRICK!
WE NEED A TREAT!
WE WOULD EVEN LET YOU
SMELL OUR FEET!"

The candy is given to the others first.
Oh, no! The best treats will be gone.
They'll leave us the worst!

We each grab a handful and get away fast.
Of course, we just can't stand to be last.

The next door doesn't open.
The porch light goes out.
Is Halloween over?
"OH NO!" we shout.

We try it again.
We scream extra loud.
"WE WANT TO TRICK! WE NEED A TREAT!
WE WOULD EVEN LET YOU SMELL OUR FEET!"

We stop and we gather.
We start counting our treasure.
Our bags are half-empty.
There is too little to measure!

The night is not over.
We need to get more.
Wait, those other trick-or-
treaters are headed to the door.
It's not going to open.
This will be fun.
We'll laugh and we'll holler
when they get none.

Lights come on brightly. The candy bowl appears.
Everyone's smiling and they're getting treats here.
Something seems crazy. Something's not right.
Something is working
for those kids tonight.

We didn't hear shouting and nobody screamed,
"WE WANT TO TRICK! WE NEED A TREAT!
WE WOULD EVEN LET YOU SMELL OUR FEET!"

They used soft voices and said thank you and please.
As each bag was filled, those kids didn't push, shove, or tease.

Let's do something different. Let's try something new.
We say to each other, "You were thinking that, too?"
Could it be that Halloween
  is not over yet?
A new plan might work
  and we'll be all set.

The next house is here and off we go,
carrying our half empty bags in tow.
Standing in line knocking softly at the door,
our voices are pleasant, and there's no shoving anymore.

"We don't want to trick.
Please give us a treat.

We know you don't want
to smell our feet."

Smiling faces
like our new rhyme.
Seems like
we thought of it
just in time.

"Thank you," we say,
as we turn to walk away.
Let's try this again.
We all say okay.

The last house on the street is up ahead.
Up the walk we go, remembering what we said.
We patiently wait for others to leave
and say our rhyme softly, taking care to please.

"We don't want to trick.
Please give us a treat.
We know you don't want
to smell our feet."

As treats fill our bags,
we hear them exclaim,
"You children are delightful,
but you're not very frightful."

"What happened to your costumes this Halloween night?"
As we look at each other,     we are surprised to see,
that children are here     where monsters used to be...

If you enjoyed *The Monsters Three*,
check out these other books written by
Rosalind Bunn and Kathleen Howard
and illustrated by Lydia Rupinski:

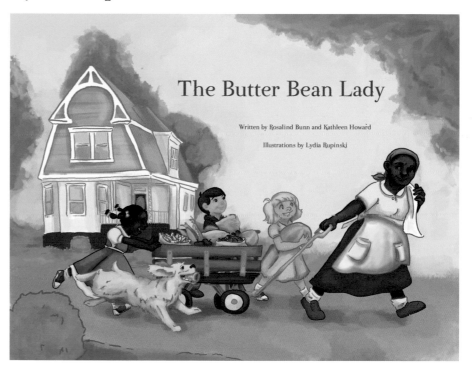

A fanciful story of Sophie May, who buys hi-top pink tennis shoes for school, but cannot tie them! The Shoe Untying Fairy plays with her laces, and gives Sophie May a rhyme to teach her how to tie those shoes! Follow her attempts as she masters this important skill, and goes on to teach a friend how to tie his shoes!

A story of love, friendship, and acceptance in Columbus, GA in the 1950s. As Dianne's grandmother buys produce from the Butter Bean Lady, the two young granddaughters have a day of play and adventure. The two families share a dinner together at the end of the day in this poignant and beautiful picture book.